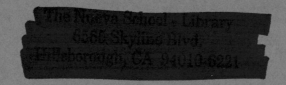

MY STARS,
IT'S MRS. GADDY!

THE THREE MRS. GADDY STORIES

by WILSON GAGE
pictures by MARYLIN HAFNER

GREENWILLOW BOOKS · NEW YORK

Library of Congress Cataloging-in-Publication Data

Gage, Wilson.
My stars, it's Mrs. Gaddy!:
the three Mrs. Gaddy stories /
by Wilson Gage;
pictures by Marylin Hafner.
      p.   cm.
Summary: Life on Mrs. Gaddy's farm is made
exciting by a ghost in her kitchen, a war with a pesky
crow, and a vine that will not stop growing.
ISBN 0-688-10514-9
[1. Farm life—Fiction.]   I. Hafner, Marylin, ill.
II. Title.   PZ7.G1224My   1991
[E]—dc20   90-47857   CIP   AC

*Again, for Libby and for Pat
and for the memory of my mother,
but most of all for Polly*

—M.Q.S.

*to Kathy, Meribah,
Max, and Chris*

—M.H.

CONTENTS

MRS. GADDY AND THE GHOST

Mrs. Gaddy was a farmer.
She had a little old house
and a big old barn.
She had some fields of corn
and a vegetable garden.
She had a meadow
and some apple trees.
She had a storm cellar to go in
if a tornado happened.
She had some chickens.
She had a cow and a mule.
It was a very nice farm.

There was only one trouble.

The little old house was haunted.

There was a ghost in the kitchen.

It made awful noises at night.

Mrs. Gaddy did not like it.

She worked very hard.

She needed lots of sleep.

The ghost kept her awake.

She could not think of any way

to get rid of that ghost.

One night Mrs. Gaddy was sleeping.

Suddenly there was a loud noise.

Thump! Thump! Thump!

Mrs. Gaddy woke up.

"Drat," she said.

"There is that ghost again.

Something must be done."

Mrs. Gaddy jumped out of bed.

She lighted her candle

and went downstairs.

She went in the kitchen

and looked all around.

"Come out!" she called.

"I know you're here.

I heard you thump!"

There was a ghosty-looking thing
high up in a corner of the kitchen.
Mrs. Gaddy got her broom
and swept it down.
She opened the back door and
swept the ghosty thing outside.
"There," she said.
"That takes care of that!"
And she went back to bed.

But a few nights later

she heard another noise.

Whooo! Whooo! Whooo!

"Drat and double drat!"

cried Mrs. Gaddy.

"That ghost has come back."

She took her candle

and went downstairs.

"Now it is in the chimney," she said.

She got some bug spray.

She sprayed and sprayed up the chimney.

"That ought to get rid of it!" she said.

And she went back to bed.

But two nights later

she heard another noise.

Clank! Clank! Clank!

"Oh, my stars!" she yelled.

"That ghost has got in the oven!"

Mrs. Gaddy ran downstairs.

"I'll fix it now," she said.

She got a lot of wood

and built a big fire in the stove.

Then she sat down to wait.

She wanted to be sure

that ghost was really cooked.

"What a nice hot fire," she said.

"I should bake some bread."

Mrs. Gaddy went to the pantry.
There was her fresh bread
rising in the pans.
She forgot about the ghost.
She brought the pans
from the pantry and
opened the oven door.
Poof!

"Oh, tarnation!" Mrs. Gaddy shouted.
"I have let that ghost out!
And what am I doing baking bread
in the middle of the night?"
She put the pans back in the pantry
and went upstairs to bed.

The next night
she heard another
awful noise.
Clump! Clump! Clump!
Mrs. Gaddy jumped
out of bed and
ran down to the kitchen.
She held up her candle.
She thought she saw
something ghosty under the table.

Mrs. Gaddy took off her slipper
and slapped the ghosty thing.
"Dang, I missed it," she said.
She slapped something ghosty
under her rocking chair.
"Missed again," said Mrs. Gaddy.
She slapped all around the kitchen.
"I will never hit that ghosty thing,"
she said. "It is too hard to see."
Suddenly something ghosty
jumped in the churn!
"Bless my soul!" Mrs. Gaddy cried.
"I have that ghost now!"

Quick as a flash she put
the lid on the churn.
She fastened the lid down tight.
"Good," said Mrs. Gaddy.
"It will never get out of that churn."
And she went back to bed.

The next day Mrs. Gaddy got up early.

She fed her animals.

"I must make my butter," said Mrs. Gaddy.

She got a pan of cream.

"Oh, my stars and garters!" she hollered.

"That ghost is in my churn.

I need butter.

I will just have to

let the ghost out."

Mrs. Gaddy took the lid off the churn
and looked inside.

There was nothing there.

"Good gravy!" she cried.

"That ghost has got out all by itself!"

Mrs. Gaddy was
really mad.
She poured
the cream
into the churn
and began
to churn it.
"I wish that ghost
was still in there,"
she said. "I would
churn it into bits.

I would make butter out of it
and feed it to my hens."
Suddenly she had an idea.
"I will set a trap for it," she said.
"I will set a mousetrap.
I will use gingerbread for bait.
Everybody likes gingerbread."

That night Mrs. Gaddy

set her mousetrap very carefully.

She used gingerbread for bait.

Then she went to bed.

She slept all night.

There were no scary noises.

Next morning Mrs. Gaddy
was very happy.
"Oh, I have caught
that ghost," she said.
She went downstairs.
The trap had been sprung.
The gingerbread was gone.
But there was nothing
in the trap.

"That ghost has got away
again!" she yelled.
"Whatever shall I do?"

Mrs. Gaddy thought and thought.
"I could spread glue
all over everything," she said.
"The glue would surely
catch the ghost.
But bless my big toe!
It would catch me too.
That would never do."

Mrs. Gaddy thought some more.

"I could move away," she said.

"Oh, I would not like that.

I have lived here a long time.

I love my little old house

and my big old barn.

I would miss my apple trees

and my chickens and my cow.

Oh dear, oh dear."

Mrs. Gaddy was very upset.

Still, she had all her work to do.
She went out to the barn
to take care of her animals.
The barn was very tidy.
There were no rats or mice.
Mrs. Gaddy had an idea.
"Maybe I can get rid of that ghost
the way my grandmother taught me
to get rid of rats and mice," she cried.
"I will try it!"

Mrs. Gaddy ran back into her house.

She got her pen and some ink

and some paper.

She wrote a letter.

It was a very polite letter.

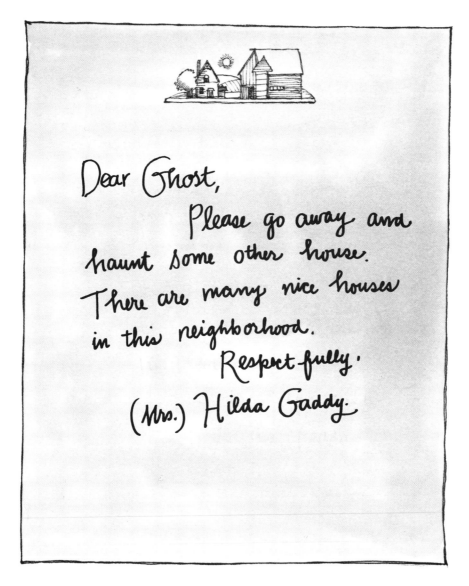

Dear Ghost,
     Please go away and
haunt some other house.
There are many nice houses
in this neighborhood.
          Respectfully,
(Mrs.) Hilda Gaddy.

That night she put the letter
on the kitchen table.
"That ghost will be sure
to see it there," she said.
Then she went to bed
and fell fast asleep.

But something
waked her
in the night.
Strange sounds
were coming
from the kitchen.

"Oh, good gravy," she said.

"That ghost is crying!

What sad sounds!

Why is it crying like that?"

Mrs. Gaddy thought a minute.

"Oh, forevermore!

What have I done?"

she asked herself.

"That ghost has lived here

longer than I have.

It feels just the way I do.

"It loves this little house.

It does not want to leave.

It wants to stay right here

in its own home."

Mrs. Gaddy jumped out of bed
and ran downstairs.
"Don't cry, ghost," she called.
"You don't have to leave.
I will tear up the letter.
Tomorrow I will go to town
and buy some earmuffs.
I will wear them when I go to bed.
Then I won't hear
all that thumping and clanking."
The ghost sniffled and snuffled.
"There, there," said Mrs. Gaddy.
"I mean it. You can stay."
Mrs. Gaddy tore up the letter
and threw it in the stove.
Then she went back to bed.
The ghost was very quiet.

Next day Mrs. Gaddy went to town.

That night when she went to bed,

she put on the earmuffs.

She could not hear a thing.

Late in the night

Mrs. Gaddy woke up.

Still she did not hear a thing.

She tossed and turned.

She counted sheep.

She couldn't get back to sleep.

Finally she sat up

and took off the earmuffs.

She could hear noises

in the kitchen.

Thump! Thump! Thump!

"What a nice noise,"
said Mrs. Gaddy.
"A ghost in the kitchen
is very good company.

"Tomorrow I will bake
some gingerbread for it.
And now I believe
I can go back to sleep."
And she did.

THE CROW
AND MRS. GADDY

One spring day Mrs. Gaddy
planted her corn.
She made furrows in the earth
and dropped in grains of corn.
Then she waited
for the corn to sprout.
She waited and waited.
Many days passed.
Nothing happened.

"Tarnation!" cried Mrs. Gaddy.

"I believe a bad crow has eaten

all my grains of corn.

Well, I know what to do about that!"

Once again Mrs. Gaddy

made furrows in the earth.

But this time she did not

drop in grains of corn.

Instead, she dropped in

round white pebbles.

Mrs. Gaddy went back to her house.

It was Monday,

and she had to do her washing.

Sure enough,

a crow flew down

from a tree.

He began to eat the pebbles.

"Ugh!" said the crow.

"These are not grains of corn!

Oh, I feel terrible!

What a mean woman.

I will get even with her!"

Mrs. Gaddy hung her clothes
on a line to dry.
"What a fine sunny day," she said.
She went into the house.
And that crow flew up and pulled
all the clothespins from the line.

Plop! Plop! Plop!

All the clean clothes fell down into the dirt.

Mrs. Gaddy looked out the window.

"Oh, my stars and garters!"
she cried.

"Look what that bad crow has done!"
But Mrs. Gaddy did not
wash the clothes again.

Instead, she baked gingerbread.

She put in lots and lots of ginger.

She also put in lots of salt
and some soap powder and pepper.

When the gingerbread
was baked, Mrs. Gaddy
put it on the windowsill
to cool.

"There," she said.

"I will have gingerbread
for my supper."

The crow saw the pan on the sill.
By and by he flew down
and took a big bite of gingerbread.

"Oooh! Blah!" croaked the crow.
"What awful gingerbread!
It tastes like salt.
It tastes like soap.

"That mean woman has played
another trick on me.
But I will get even with her!"
He looked all around.
Mrs. Gaddy's knitting
was lying on a table.
The crow grabbed the yarn
and pulled and pulled and pulled.

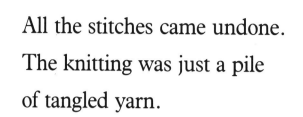

All the stitches came undone.
The knitting was just a pile
of tangled yarn.

"Oh, my stars and stockings!"
yelled Mrs. Gaddy. "That bad crow
has unknitted my sweater!
Well, I will teach him a good lesson."

Mrs. Gaddy went to town.
She bought some balloons.
That night she blew them up.

In the dark she went outside
and tied the balloons
all over her apple tree.

The next morning Mrs. Gaddy
looked out her window.
"My, what lovely apples!" she shouted.
"I hope that crow doesn't peck them."

Right away the crow flew
to the apple tree.
He gave one of the balloons
a really hard peck.
POW! went the balloon.
"Ow!" went the crow. "That hurt.
What a mean woman.
But I can get even with her."

Mrs. Gaddy went to the barn.

The crow found a big black beetle.

Mrs. Gaddy came out of the barn

with a pail of milk.

The crow flew over and dropped

the beetle right into the milk.

Mrs. Gaddy's good fresh milk was spoiled.

She was mad.

"But I will teach that crow

a lesson," she said.

Every day Mrs. Gaddy played

a new trick on the crow.

Every day the crow played

a new trick

on Mrs. Gaddy.

The crow was so busy,
he did not have time
to find a wife.
He did not have time
to raise a family.

Mrs. Gaddy was so busy,
she did not have time
to work in her garden.
She did not have time
to keep her house
clean and tidy.

One day she went into her garden
to get some beans for supper.
"Oh, bless my big toe!"
cried Mrs. Gaddy.
"What a horrible mess!
Look at all those weeds!
Look at all those bugs
eating my tomatoes!"

She hoed and weeded and raked.
At the end of the day
she was very tired.
She went right to bed
and slept and slept.

The sun rose the next morning,
and still Mrs. Gaddy was sleeping.
The crow looked in her window
to see what was the matter.
Mrs. Gaddy was sleeping.
Her glasses were on
the table beside her bed.
"Goody," said the crow.
"I will fix that old woman.
I will steal her glasses!"

51

The crow flew in the window
and picked up the glasses.
Mrs. Gaddy woke up.
She sat up in bed.
"Who's there?" she cried.
The crow was scared.
Instead of flying out the window,
he flew down the stairs.
"Who's there?"
Mrs. Gaddy yelled again.
"Where are my glasses?"
Maybe I left my glasses
in the kitchen,
thought Mrs. Gaddy.

She put on her slippers
and went down the stairs.
She could barely see.
She went into the kitchen.

The crow was perched on the stove.
"Oh, drat and drat!"
cried Mrs. Gaddy.
"My kitchen is a mess.
I have wasted so much time
with that bad crow.
I should have been scrubbing
my kitchen and tending my garden.
Oh, look at that big black smut
on my nice stove!"

Mrs. Gaddy grabbed her feather duster.

She tried to dust the crow
off the stove.
"What a big smut!" she cried.
"I can't dust it away."

She grabbed a pail
of soap and water.
She threw it on the crow.
"That horrid smut!
It won't go away,"
shouted Mrs. Gaddy.

She picked up the fire tongs
and snapped them at the smut.
The tongs closed over
the crow's tail feathers.
"What a big smut,"
said Mrs. Gaddy.
She opened the door
and threw the crow outside.

The crow landed in a rosebush.

"What a mean woman," he croaked.

"She is trying to kill me.

First she nearly tickled me to death.

Then she tried to drown me.

And now I am stuck

in this rosebush.

I don't think I will try

to get even with her again."

Mrs. Gaddy went back upstairs.

She got dressed

and put on her best hat.

She was going to town

to buy some new glasses.

"I am a stupid woman," she cried.

"I was so dumb to waste my time

teaching that crow a lesson.

Now my house is dirty

and my garden is full of weeds.

"I should have made a scarecrow
instead of baking gingerbread
with soap in it."
Mrs. Gaddy began to laugh.
"Ha! Ha! Ha! It was so funny
when he ate that awful stuff.
Next time I will bake a pie
filled with hot peppers.
I bet that will teach him!"

The crow climbed
out of the rosebush.
He was all scratched up.
His feathers were wet.
He had no wife or children
to comfort him.
"I have been really dumb," he said.
"I have wasted all summer
getting even with that mean woman.
I wasted my time finding
a beetle to drop in her milk."

The crow scratched his head.

"Ho! Ho! Ho!" he croaked.

"That really made me laugh.

Next time I will find

a snake to drop in her milk pail!

I bet that will fix her."

Just then the crow heard Mrs. Gaddy.

She was laughing. "Ha! Ha! Ha!"

"Oh, oh," said the crow.

"I bet that mean woman

has thought of a really awful trick

to play on me.

I wonder what it is.

I don't think I'll wait to see."

And he dried his feathers
and flew away to look for a snake.
Just in case.

MRS. GADDY AND THE FAST-GROWING VINE

Mrs. Gaddy grew many fruits
and vegetables.
She raised cherries and apples
and strawberries.
But Mrs. Gaddy loved flowers.
So she also grew roses
and lilies and snapdragons
and black-eyed Susans.

One day Mrs. Gaddy went out

to pick some roses.

"Oh, my!" she cried.

"Everything looks so pretty.

There is just one bare spot

by the kitchen door.

I think I need a vine to grow there."

Mrs. Gaddy went to the barn.

She hitched her mule to her wagon.

She drove to town.

In the market a man was selling plants.

"Do you have a vine for sale?"

asked Mrs. Gaddy.

"I want a vine that will grow fast.

I want a vine with pretty flowers."

"Here is just the thing,"
said the salesman. "This vine
has pretty purple flowers, and
it grows as fast as lightning."
When Mrs. Gaddy got home,
she planted the new vine.

The next morning

she hurried out to look at it.

"My stars!" she cried. "Here is

a new green shoot already.

What a fast vine!"

Mrs. Gaddy went about her chores.

That afternoon she looked again.

The shoot had grown.

It was as tall as she was.

"Good!" said Mrs. Gaddy. "This vine

will soon cover that bare spot."

Next morning when she woke up,
she saw something at her window.
"Good gravy!" she yelled.
"That vine is trying
to come in my window."
She got her pruning shears
and went outside.
"Oh, my stars and stuffing!"
shouted Mrs. Gaddy.

The vine now had three shoots.
One was growing
in Mrs. Gaddy's bedroom window.
One was coiling around the chimney.
One was curling over the roof.

Mrs. Gaddy pruned all three shoots.
"There," she said. "That ought
to slow it down."

But that afternoon the vine
had four new shoots.
Mrs. Gaddy cut all the shoots
down to the ground.
But two days later the vine
had grown again.
It was bigger than ever.

"My sainted snakes!"
cried Mrs. Gaddy. "This vine
is trying to eat me alive."

She got an ax and chopped
and chopped the vine.
"That fixed it," she said.
"I will buy a rosebush
to plant in that bare spot."

But during the night
that vine started growing again.
Mrs. Gaddy tried to dig it up.
But the roots went too deep
into the ground. The vine
just went on growing.
Soon Mrs. Gaddy's house
was covered with   that vine.

The leaves grew over the windows.
The stalks grew across
the kitchen door.
She could hardly get through it.
Mrs. Gaddy was at her wits' end.

"This vine is swallowing my house,"
she said. "Soon it will swallow me
and my mule and my cow.
What shall I do?"

Mrs. Gaddy poured
boiling water on the vine.
But it went on growing.
She poured molasses on it.
"Molasses is so slow," she said.
"And it is sticky. Surely molasses
will slow down this vine."
But the vine sent up
more long green shoots.

Mrs. Gaddy sprinkled it
with salt and pepper and mustard.
But the vine went on growing.
Mrs. Gaddy piled stones on the vine.
But the vine just grew around them.
She put her big soup pot over it.
But new shoots just wriggled
out from under the pot.

"Oh, tarnation!" said Mrs. Gaddy.

Suddenly she had an idea.

She hitched her mule

to her wagon

and drove to town.

In the market

a man was selling goats.

"Are these goats good eaters?"

asked Mrs. Gaddy.

"These goats can eat a bulldozer,"

said the salesman.

"Then sell me the one

with the biggest appetite!"

cried Mrs. Gaddy.

When Mrs. Gaddy got home,
she led the goat up to the vine.
"Now, eat!" she told it.
The goat ate.

It ate all the leaves.
It ate all the flowers.
Every time a new shoot sprang up,
the goat ate it.

It ate and ate.

It dug up the ground

with its sharp hooves.

It ate all the roots.

Mrs. Gaddy watched closely.

There were no more green shoots.

"Oh, what a good goat!" she cried.

"I think you have done for that vine!"

"Baaah!" said the goat,

and rolled its yellow eyes.

"But bless my big toe!"

said Mrs. Gaddy. "What will

I do with this goat now?"

The goat began to eat a rosebush.
"Stop that!" yelled Mrs. Gaddy.
The goat finished the rosebush
and began to eat a lilac.
"Now, you quit that!"
screamed Mrs. Gaddy.
She stamped her foot. The goat
ate a whole row of snapdragons.

"I'll chase it into the barn
with my broom," Mrs. Gaddy said.
She went to get a broom.
While Mrs. Gaddy was gone,
the goat ran around the house.
Mrs. Gaddy's front door stood open.

The goat walked in.

It ate some flowers in a vase.

It ate a lampshade.

It began to eat the rug.

Mrs. Gaddy came out
the kitchen door.
She waved her broom.
"Now, where has that goat gone?"
she wondered. "I hope it has gone
a long way from here.
As long as I have my broom,
I will sweep the front steps."

Mrs. Gaddy went around her house.

She saw the open door.

She saw the goat eating her rug.

"Oh, my stars and stockings!"

she yelled.

She chased the goat out of the house.

She chased it into the barn.

The goat began to eat some hay.

"Whatever shall I do?" cried Mrs. Gaddy.

"I can't let this awful goat

eat all the hay and oats.

How would I feed my mule?

And my cow?"

The goat ate and ate.

Mrs. Gaddy brought it some green beans and
some potatoes and some gingerbread.

It ate them all and looked around for more.

"I could lock it in my storm cellar,"
said Mrs. Gaddy.

"There is nothing to eat there.

But then it would starve.

I can't let it starve."

She thought and thought.
"Maybe I could buy another vine
for it to eat," she said.
Suddenly she had an idea.
She hitched her mule
to her wagon.

She put a lot of gingerbread
in the wagon.
The goat jumped in the wagon
to eat the gingerbread.
Mrs. Gaddy jumped in too.
She drove to town.

She saw the man who had
sold the vine to her.

"Have you sold any more
  of those vines?"
  asked Mrs. Gaddy.
"Oh, yes," said the salesman.
"Mrs. Green bought one
  just this morning.
  She wanted a vine
  to grow on her fence."
  Mrs. Gaddy drove on.
  She drove very fast.
  The goat had eaten
  all the gingerbread.
  It began to eat the wagon seat.
  Very soon they came
  to Mrs. Green's house.

"Oh, Mrs. Gaddy," said Mrs. Green.
"Look at this vine.
  I have just planted it, and
  already it has put up a shoot."
"I have brought you a present,
  Mrs. Green," said Mrs. Gaddy.
  She got out of the wagon.
  The goat got out of the wagon.

Mrs. Gaddy tied the goat
to the fence.
"That is very kind of you,
but I really don't need a goat,"
said Mrs. Green.
Mrs. Gaddy looked at the vine.
Another shoot was sprouting.
"I think you need a goat
very badly," she said.

She got back in her wagon
and drove away.
"I will plant a rosebush
in that bare spot,"
Mrs. Gaddy said to herself.
"Roses grow slowly.
But there is no need
to be in such a hurry.
It only leads to trouble!"

pay for some of the expenses incurred in converting a portion of your land to an efficient woodlot.

In addition, you might write:

> The American Tree Farm System
> American Forest Institute
> 1619 Massachusetts Avenue, N.W.
> Washington, D.C. 20036

They will provide you with a wealth of information and technical advice. Just remember they are industry oriented, rather than consumer oriented, and you will have to wade through a certain amount of self-serving chitchat.